Titles in our Stories Without Words series:
The Chicken Thief by Béatrice Rodriguez
Fox and Hen Together by Béatrice Rodriguez
Rooster's Revenge by Béatrice Rodriguez
Ice by Arthur Geisert
The Giant Seed by Arthur Geisert

www.enchantedlionbooks.com

First American Edition published in 2014 by Enchanted Lion Books, 351 Van Brunt Street, Brooklyn, NY 11231

Library of Congress Control Number: 2013952473
ISBN: 978-1-59270-147-6
Printed in November 2013 in China by South China Printing Co. Ltd.

Coyote Run

GAËTAN DORÉMUS

ENCHANTED LION BOOKS
NEW YORK

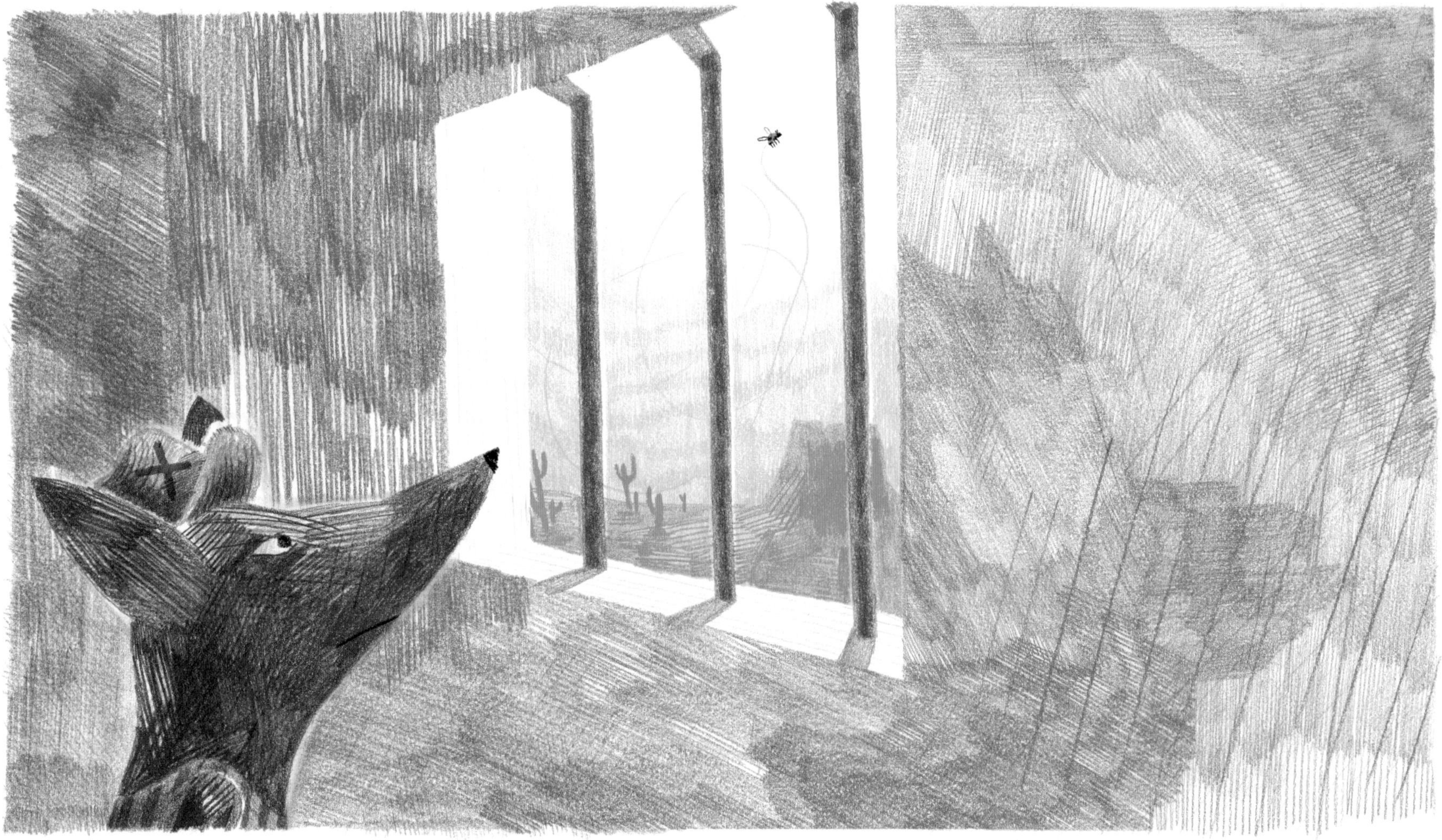